SHARE A STORY

D0186670

THIS IS THE BEAR

Introduction

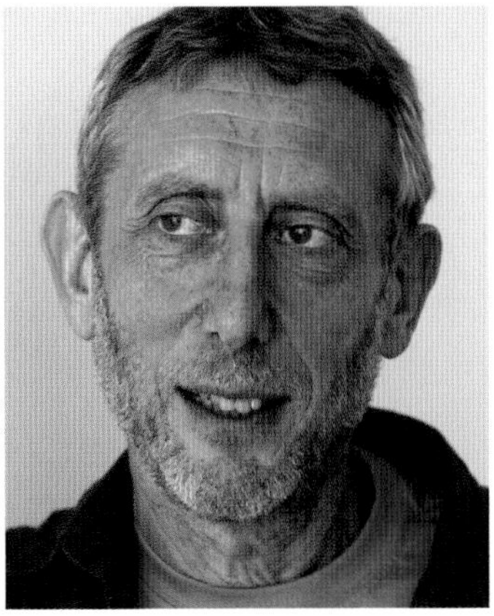

One of the best ways you can help your children learn and learn to read is to share books with them. Here's why:

- They get to know the **sounds**, **rhythms** and **words** used in the way we write. This is different from how we talk, so hearing stories helps children learn how to read.

- They think about the **feelings** of the characters in the book. This helps them as they go about their own lives with other people.

- They think about the **ideas** in the book. This helps them to understand the world.

- Sharing books and listening to what your children say about them shows your children that you care about them, you care about what they think and who they are.

Michael Rosen

Michael Rosen
Writer and Poet
Children's Laureate (2007-9)

For Barbara, who makes bears
S.H.

For Edward (Teddy) Craig
H.C.

First published 1986 by Walker Books Ltd
87 Vauxhall Walk, London SE11 5HJ

This edition published 2011

2 4 6 8 10 9 7 5 3 1

This book has been typeset in ITC Garamond Light

Printed in China

British Library Cataloguing in Publication Data:
a catalogue record for this book is available from the British Library

ISBN 978-1-4063-3496-8

www.walker.co.uk

THIS IS THE BEAR

Written by
Sarah Hayes

Illustrated by
Helen Craig

WALKER BOOKS
AND SUBSIDIARIES
LONDON • BOSTON • SYDNEY • AUCKLAND

I'm Fred.

This is the bear

who fell in the bin.

Oh no!
Oh dear!

This is the dog
who pushed him in.

This is heavy.
Fred's in there!

This is the man

who picked up the sack.

Let's go.
Stop, stop!

This is the driver

who would not come back.

This is the bear
who went to the dump

Ouch!

and fell on the pile
with a bit of a bump.

This is the boy

who took the bus

Find my bear!
You must be joking.

and went to the dump
to make a fuss.

Not here!

This is the man
in an awful grump

Not there?

who searched and searched
and searched the dump.

This is the bear
all cold and cross

Here I am.

who did not think
he was really lost.

This is the dog
who smelled the smell

Yum, yum.

of a bone

What's this?

and a tin

Hello, Fred.

and a bear as well.

I must be mad.
TED 86

This is the man
who drove them home –

I'm the champ.
Good dog.
TED 86

the boy, the bear

and the dog with a bone.

This is the bear
all lovely and clean

A little trip.

who did not say
just where he had been.

Don't tell.
I won't.

This is the boy

who knew quite well,

I will.

but promised his friend

he would not tell.

And this is the boy
who woke up in the night
and asked the bear
if he felt all right –
and was very surprised
when the bear shouted out,
“How soon can we have
another day out?”

Sharing Stories

Sharing stories together is a pleasurable way to help children learn to read and enjoy books. Reading stories aloud and encouraging children to talk about the pictures and join in with parts of the story they know well are good ways to build their interest in books. They will want to share their favourite books again and again. This is an important part of becoming a successful reader.

Oh no!
Oh dear!

This Is the Bear is a gentle story of the rivalry between the two most important friends in a boy's life: his dog and his teddy bear. Many children will be able to relate the story to their own experiences with friends or siblings. Here are some ways you can share this book:

- As you read the book together the first time, use the pictures to help your child to predict what might happen next.

- The strong rhythm and rhyme really help you to read this story in a lively way. After reading it aloud a few times, encourage your child to join in with the rhyming word or phrase, leaving space for them to say it.

- This is a book in which the words and pictures tell different parts of the story. Children can tell it to you in their own words, turning the pages and using the pictures to prompt them.

- Talking together is a good way to deepen children's enjoyment of the book, their understanding of the story and the way it is written. For example:

  "Why would the dog want to put the bear in the bin?"

  " 'Ouch!' says the bear – it's just like your comic."

  "Why do you think the man was 'in an awful grump'?"

  "I wonder why the bear didn't say where he'd been."

- At the end of the book, the bear decides he wants to have another day out. Children can imagine what kind of adventure the bear has next, then tell and draw their own story.

SHARE A STORY

A First Reading Programme

From Pre-school to School

Beginnings – 2 years+
Look Out, Suzy Goose
Petr Horáček
Walking Through the Jungle
Julie Lacome
Hello, Goodbye
David Lloyd
Louise Voce
Penny Dale
TEN IN THE BED
THIS IS THE BEAR
Sarah Hayes Helen Craig
The Big Wide-Mouthed Frog
Early Steps – 3 years+
A New House for Mouse
Petr Horacek
The Train Ride
June Crebbin
Stephen Lambert
THE OTHER DAY I MET A BEAR
Old MacDonald Had a Farm
The Tiger and the Jackal
Vivian French
Alison Bartlett
Zed's Bread
Mick Manning Brita Granström
Next Steps – 4 years+
The Hairy Toe
Daniel Postgate
The True Story of Humpty Dumpty
Sarah Hayes
Charlotte Voake
BEANS ON TOAST
Paul Dowling
Over in the Meadow
A Counting Rhyme
Louise Voce
Polly Dunbar
Dog Blue
Night-night, Knight
And Other Poems
Michael Rosen
Sue Heap
Taking Off – 5 years+
"Have You Seen the Crocodile?"
Colin West
HANDA'S SURPRISE
Eileen Browne
The Ravenous Beast
Niamh Sharkey
Allan Ahlberg
Colin McNaughton
One, Two, Flea!
Nick Sharratt
Dinosaurs' Day Out
The Old Woman and the Red Pumpkin
Introduced by Michael Rosen

Sharing the best books makes the best readers

WALKER BOOKS

www.walker.co.uk